When Wishes Were Horses

by Sharon Hart Addy
Illustrated by Brad Sneed

Houghton Mifflin Company   Boston 2002

Library of Congress Cataloging-in-Publication Data

Addy, Sharon Hart.
When wishes were horses / written by Sharon Hart Addy; illustrated by Brad Sneed.
p. cm.
Summary: On a hot, dusty day as Zeb is walking to the general store, he wishes for
a horse, but soon his one horse grows into a snorting, stamping herd.
ISBN 0-618-13166-3
[1. Horses—Fiction. 2. Wishes—Fiction.] I. Sneed, Brad, ill. II. Title.
PZ7.A257 Wh 2002
[E]—dc21   00-050035

Printed in Singapore
TWP 10 9 8 7 6 5 4 3 2 1

For G, who believed
—S. H. A.

For my dad, the horseman
—B. S.

One day in the town of Dusty Gulch, Zeb's ma sent him to Goody's General Store for flour.

The sack was heavy, and the sun beat down something fierce. Zeb pushed his hat back to wipe his forehead. "Sure wish it wasn't so hot," he mumbled.

When the wind stirred up a parcel of dust and made Zeb sneeze, he said, "I sure wish it wasn't so dry."

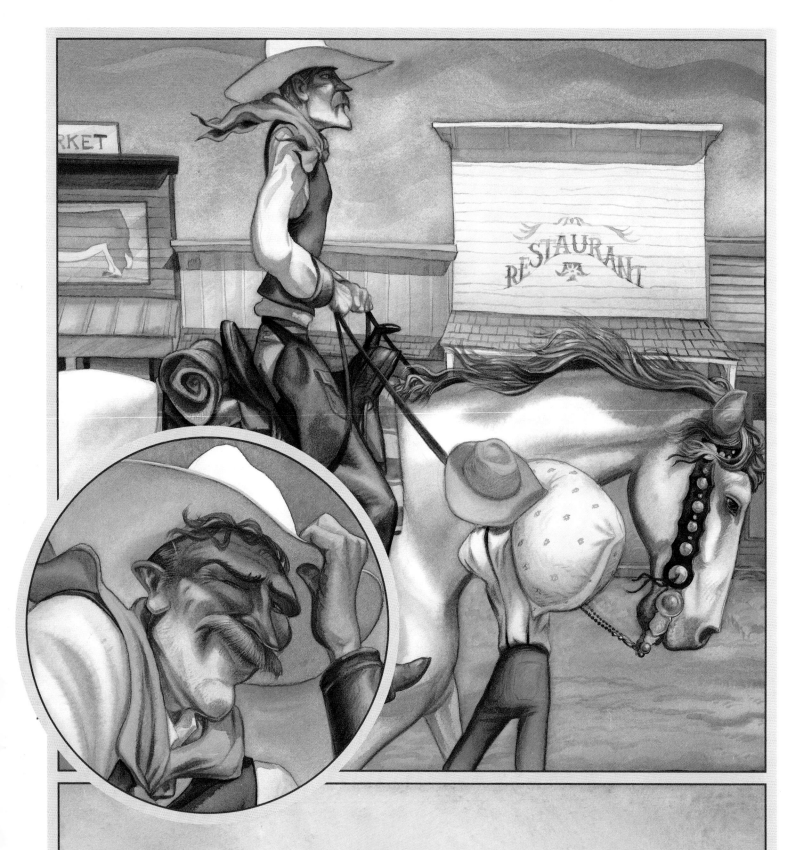

When a cowhand rode past, Zeb said, "I wish I had a horse. I wish, I wish, I wish I had a horse."

The cowhand glanced back at Zeb, winked, and tipped his white Stetson.

Zeb tipped his hat in return. Then he felt a nudge on his shoulder. Something warm brushed his ear. He turned his head and found himself eye to eye with a buckskin cow pony.

With a loud "Yahoo!" Zeb flung that sack of flour over the buckskin's back, climbed on, and rode home bareback.

He ran into the kitchen. "Ma," he yelled, "I got myself a horse. I wished it up!"

Ma shook her head. "Horse-feathers! Don't bother me with your wishing foolishment. I'm in the middle of bread-making."

Zeb slumped off, muttering, "I wish you'd—" And right then, in the boarding-house kitchen, a palomino with a white blaze appeared.

The palomino neighed and snorted, backed into the hot cast-iron stove, upset the kitchen table, and tore the door off its hinges on its way out.

Zeb took one look at the vexation on Ma's face and followed the palomino.

Outside he had another thought. *Two horses.
If I catch him I got two horses.*

That palomino hightailed it down Main Street
at breakneck speed. It thundered past the hotel,
completely discombobulating Mrs. Vander
Snooty, who was stepping off the stagecoach.

"Well, I do declare!" Mrs. Vander Snooty snooted. She rammed her hat back in place and grabbed Zeb as he pounded past.

"Young man," she snapped at him. "Have you no sense of responsibility? I could have been trampled. I could have been—"

Zeb pulled away. "Ma'am, I've got to catch that horse. I'm sorry. I wish it hadn't—"

And faster than you can say "howdy," a chestnut
mare stood nose to nose with Mrs. Vander Snooty.
Mrs. Vander Snooty fainted dead away.

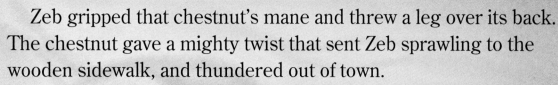

Zeb gripped that chestnut's mane and threw a leg over its back. The chestnut gave a mighty twist that sent Zeb sprawling to the wooden sidewalk, and thundered out of town.

Mr. Goody, the proprietor of the General Store, leaned on his broom, laughing. "What's the matter, son? Lose your mount?"

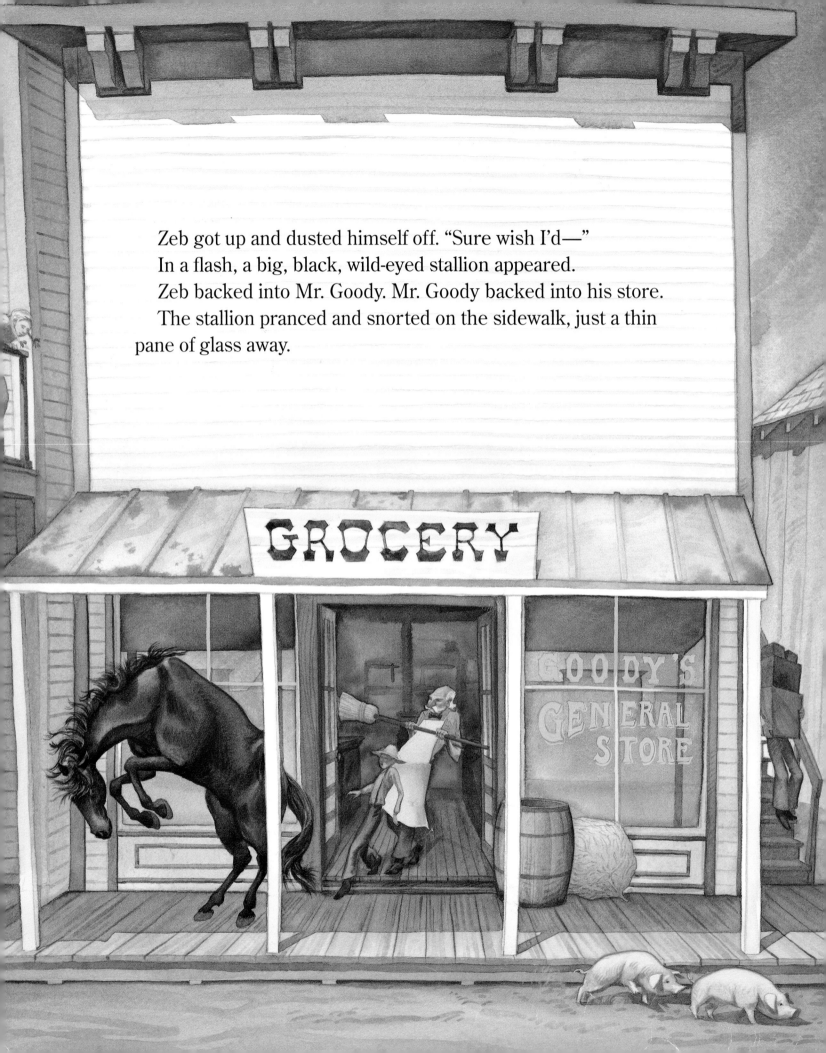

Zeb got up and dusted himself off. "Sure wish I'd—"
In a flash, a big, black, wild-eyed stallion appeared.
Zeb backed into Mr. Goody. Mr. Goody backed into his store.
The stallion pranced and snorted on the sidewalk, just a thin
pane of glass away.

Mr. Goody nudged Zeb. "Do something."
Zeb croaked, "I wish—" He slapped a hand over his mouth,
but it was too late to stop the words.

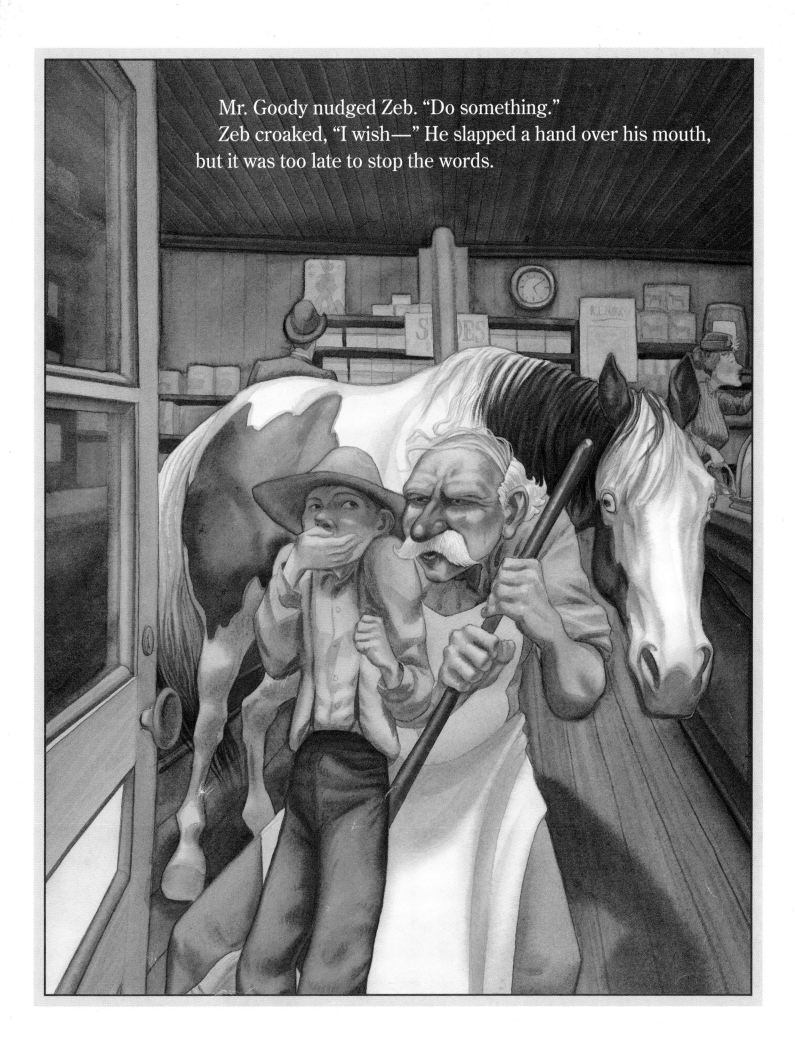

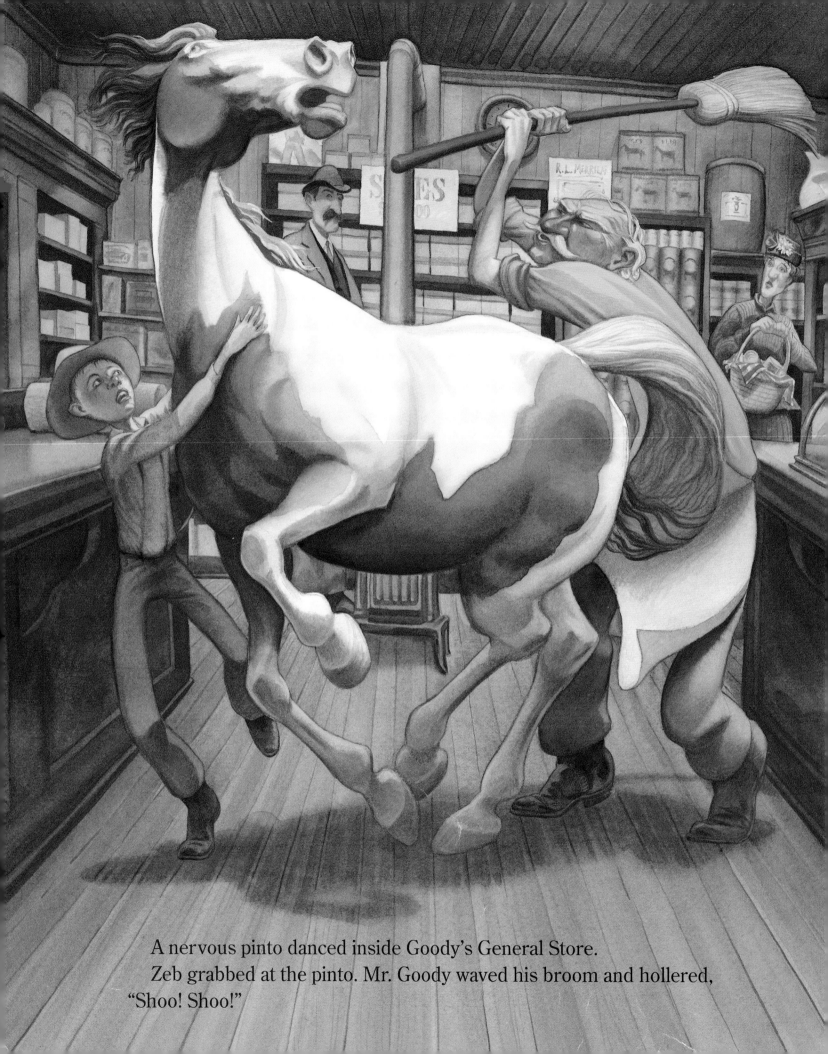

A nervous pinto danced inside Goody's General Store.
Zeb grabbed at the pinto. Mr. Goody waved his broom and hollered,
"Shoo! Shoo!"

The pinto kicked open the pickle barrel, knocked the dress mannequin through the window, and sent the store's supply of jawbreakers rolling before it vamoosed through the open door.

Mr. Goody shook his broom at Zeb. "You mischief maker! You rascal! You scoundrel! You—"

Zeb took off running.

On the far end of town, Zeb collapsed on the schoolhouse steps. He took off his hat and wiped his brow. It was all too much. Too many people yelling. Too much damage. He shook his head and said, "I'm sorry. I wish—"

A bay stood next to him, nipping grass and swinging its tail.

Zeb glared at the bay. "Maybe," he said, "I can wear out this wishing. I wish, I wish, I wish, I wish I could wear out this wishing."

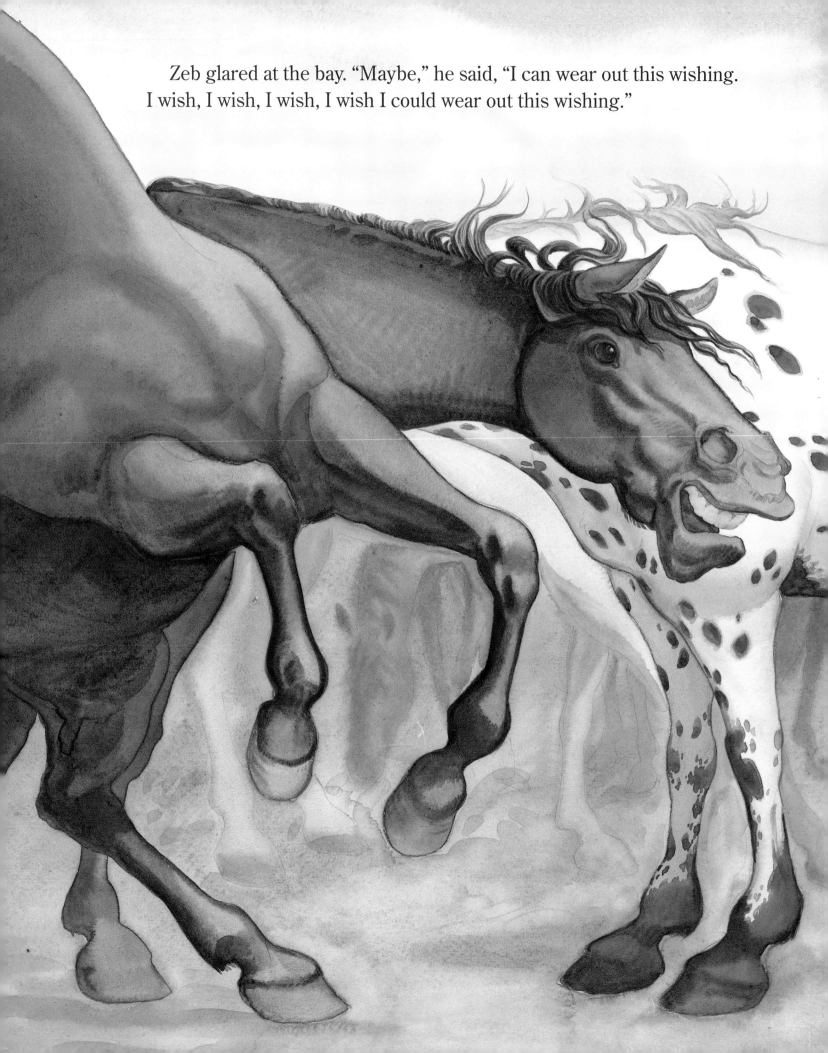

Horses milled around Zeb. The herd grew as Zeb wished on. Hooves stamped and pawed the ground. Tails swished. Muzzles snorted and whinnied.

Dust roiled around Zeb so thick he could barely breathe. Zeb stood tall, clenched his fists, and said, "I wish my wishes could just be wishes."

One by one, with a slight popping sound, the horses disappeared. When Zeb opened his eyes, he was alone. He gave a great sigh of relief.

He wondered if he was done with that foolishment. He had to know, so he whispered, "I wish."

The breeze swirled a dust devil in the distance. But that was all.

In a stronger voice, he tried again. "I wish."
Tumbleweed brushed his leg and rolled away.
But that was all.

"I wish!" he shouted. The wind pulled at his shirt and continued on its way. And that was all. With a loud "Yahoo!" Zeb jumped for joy.

A rider on the horizon waved his white Stetson in a salute.
Zeb waved his hat in return.

Then, whistling a merry tune, he put one foot in front of the other and commenced to walk home.